The Ballad of Uncle Morgan

PAGE PUBLISHING, INC.
New York, NY

First originally published by Page Publishing, Inc. 2017

ISBN 978-1-63568-943-3 (Paperback)
ISBN 978-1-63568-944-0 (Digital)

Printed in the United States of America

The Ballad of Uncle Morgan

To: Eleanor & Ezra,
Here's to Adventure!

Debra S. Carlisle Smith

Debra S. Carlisle Smith

"Who wants to go for a boat ride?" asked Jesse. Jesse's Dad had taught him to run the motor boat when he turned twelve. He let Jesse and his eight-year-old sister Annie take the small boat up the river to the sandbar.

"Come on, Annie, I'll help you buckle your life jacket," said Jesse, as they headed for the boat. Their dogs Zena and Joey scrambled. They loved going *anywhere* that Jesse and Annie went. A boat ride would be a delightful way to enjoy this lazy summer day.

Zena is a fearless and high-spirited miniature pinscher who loves chasing chipmunks and gleefully exploring the outside world. Surprisingly, she loves snuggling with Annie and Jesse just as much as she loves her outdoor adventures. Joey is a very clever chihuahua. He adores his family and protecting them is his pride and joy. Joey is Zena's big brother, and he tries his best to keep her out of danger.

Jesse, Annie, and the two dogs settled into the boat. Mom had given them lemonade and peanut butter sandwiches to snack on. The day was warm and sunny, ideal for a trip up the beautiful Muskegon River. Jesse started the motor and off they went.

Turtles were basking on logs at the edge of the river. A little side channel was filled with green lily pads and white water lilies. A family of ducks were swimming near the shore. Kingfisher birds were diving into the water, searching for food. What a great day for a boat ride!

Zena and Joey stretched out on the front deck of the boat. It was the perfect spot to scan the sandbars for frogs and turtles. Zena and Joey loved to run along the sandbars watching the startled frogs jump into the water.

Suddenly, the boat hit an underwater log! It lurched forward sending Zena and Joey into the deep water. Frantic, they swam as the current threatened to carry them down the river, far away from the boat. At last, they made it to the shore dazed and afraid. Without thinking, the two dogs took off running as fast as they could into the forest.

As Zena and Joey were running, they came upon a group of sleeping deer. Alarmed by the noise, the deer jumped up and ran. Zena knew about deer. She often saw them around the pond in their backyard. They were gentle. Maybe they would lead her safely home. Zena decided to follow the deer. Faster and faster she ran, following the deer and disappearing deeper into the woods.

Jesse and Annie quickly grabbed the small boat and dragged it up onto the sandbar. They were terrified to see that the dogs had already disappeared.

"Yip!" cried Joey. He had stepped on a huge thorn! Limping and scared, he slowly wandered back to the sandbar. Luckily, he spotted the boat. His tail wagged thankfully as he saw Annie nearby.

"Oh, Joey!" cried Annie. "Are you okay?" She gently picked him up and sat him on her lap. Carefully, she removed the nasty thorn. Joey's tail wagged and he licked Annie's face and hands. Joey was so happy that the pain from that awful thorn was gone.

"Where's your sister, Joey? Where's Zena?" asked Annie. Jesse and Annie started calling, "**Zena! Zeennaaaaa!**" They listened and heard nothing.

Annie began to feel frightened. The forest was thick, and Zena was a very little dog. If they didn't find her before dark, Annie couldn't bear to even think about it. She knew about the wild animals that lived in the forest. Her eyes welled up with tears. "What if Zena had fallen into the river and the current had swept her away?" **"Zena! she cried. Zeennaaaaa!"** Quite frantic now, Annie and Jesse were thrashing around the edge of the river searching every nook and cranny.

Suddenly, Jesse stopped. He had an idea. He remembered a story that Dad had told them many times. It was about Dad and his beloved floppy-eared hound dog, Uncle Morgan. Once, Dad and Uncle Morgan got lost in a forest on a hunting trip. Dad was very worried because it was getting dark. Then, Dad started thinking about Uncle Morgan's special way of sending a message. Dad knew that Uncle Morgan was a *baying* hound dog. That meant he *loved* howling—long, dramatic, and, sometimes, very humorous howls. Dad was able to get Uncle Morgan to howl; that magical musical howl. **It was so loud** it echoed halfway through the Manistee National Forest! Uncle Morgan howled until help came. Dad was so happy Uncle Morgan had saved the day!

Uncle Morgan became well known for his dramatic and musical howl. Jesse and Annie loved that story! They tried to teach Joey to howl when he was a puppy. It was so cute to see the little chihuahua with his tiny little voice trying to howl. It wasn't very loud and it was kind of squeaky, but he sure did try. They soon decided that maybe Joey was the wrong kind of dog for a musical howl. Maybe it was a talent that only hound dogs had.

"We've got to try *something*!" Jesse called out to Annie. "Do you remember that story that Dad use to tell us about Uncle Morgan?" he asked.

"*Yes!*" exclaimed Annie, looking up hopefully.

Jesse continued, "Maybe I can *get Joey to howl* a message to Zena! Even if it's a tiny howl, maybe Zena will hear it and try to find her way back to us."

It had been over a year since they had tried to get Joey to howl. Would he remember? Jesse petted Joey. "It's up to you boy," he said. "Do you remember how to *howl*?" Joey's ears perked up.

"Howl, boy, howl, Joey!" cried Jesse.

"Howl, Joey! Please howl!" Annie joined in.

Joey sat straight up. He did remember that word! Joey pushed his nose up toward the sky. He puckered his lips together in the shape of a little *O*, and then, he took a really big breath. "**Aawwoooo ooo ooo ooo!**" howled Joey.

"Whoa! Did Joey do that?" thought Jesse excitedly. "Joey had found his howl! It was a bit more like a yodel, but this might just work!

"Aawwoooo ooo ooo ooo!" howled Joey, again and again.

Suddenly, Zena stopped running. The deer were getting farther and farther away.

"Where am I?" she thought. "And what was that *weird* noise?"

"Aawwoooo ooo ooo ooo!" echoed through the trees.

"Joey? Could that be Joey? Joey sounds like he's in trouble!" Zena ran toward the noise, faster and faster. "He must be miles and miles away!"

Annie and Jesse sat on the sandbar near the boat looking very weary. The sun was beating down on them. Twenty minutes had passed and no sign of Zena. Annie's voice was getting very weak, and she could no longer call out. Jesse was so tired from wading through the water and searching through the brush. Joey knew it was up to him now. He continued to howl, "**Aawwoooo ooo ooo ooo! Aawwoooo ooo ooo ooo!**"

"*Listen*!" said Annie intently. "I hear something." Jesse and Annie heard leaves rustling, very faintly. Then, the sound of branches breaking, getting louder. Joey's ears stood up to listen. "Could it be?"

Jesse called out again, "**Zeennaaaaa!**" The brush parted, and there stood Zena, covered in mud and panting heavily.

With not another step left in her, Zena fell onto the sand-bar. Jesse walked over and gently picked her up stroking her head. "It's okay now, Zena. It's okay. You're safe now." Jesse sighed with relief. Jesse carefully placed Zena in Annie's arms.

"Zena, oh, Zena! We were so afraid that we'd never see you again!" whispered Annie, choking back tears and cuddling the muddy little Zena ever so tight.

Annie and Jesse hugged Joey. "*Good boy*, Joey! Your howl-ing brought Zena back to us! *Good boy*!"

"You're my hero, Joey!" exclaimed Annie. Joey's tail was wagging. He was so happy!

Then, they all got into the boat and headed down the river toward home. Zena snuggled into Annie's lap and soon fell asleep. Joey sat contentedly on the deck of the boat howling his musical, magical howl all the way home. "***Aawwoooo ooo ooo ooo!***"

About the Author

Debra S. Carlisle Smith lives in North Muskegon, Michigan. She enjoys taking leisurely boat rides on the Muskegon River with her husband Dixon and their dogs, Zena and Joey. Debra also finds joy in playing the piano or reading a good book.

Debra belonged to the White Lake Michigan Toastmasters Club for eight years. She discovered that she loved writing about true stories and weaving them into humorous adventures for children.

CPSIA information can be obtained
at www.ICGtesting.com
Printed in the USA
LVOW06s1117241217
560709LV00008B/29/P

9 781635 6894